LEVEL **1** SCIENCE
LET'S READ
AND
FIND OUT

A NEST FULL OF EGGS

BY PRISCILLA BELZ JENKINS

ILLUSTRATED BY LIZZY ROCKWELL

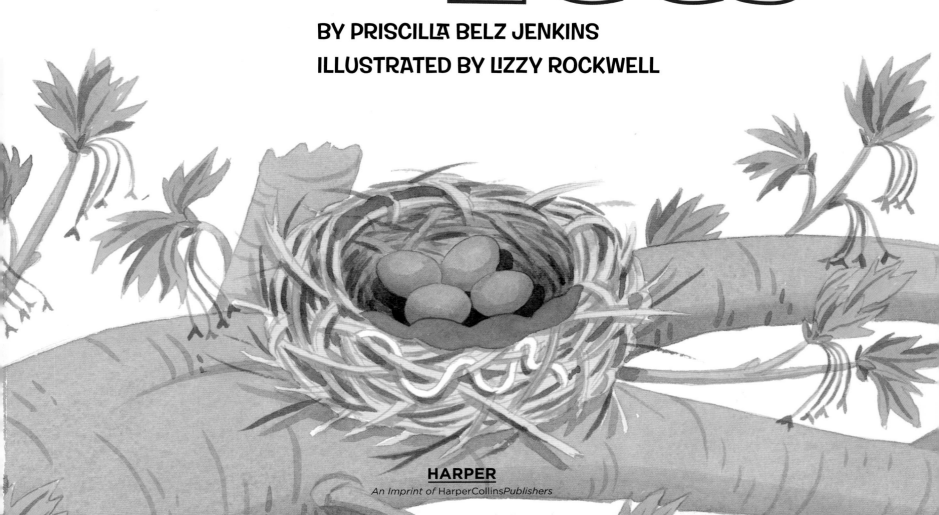

HARPER
An Imprint of HarperCollinsPublishers

To my mother, with love—P.B.J.
For Ken—L.R.

Special thanks to Dr. Charles Walcott for his expert advice.

The Let's-Read-and-Find-Out Science book series was originated by Dr. Franklyn M. Branley, Astronomer Emeritus and former Chairman of the American Museum of Natural History–Hayden Planetarium, and was formerly co-edited by him and Dr. Roma Gans, Professor Emeritus of Childhood Education, Teachers College, Columbia University. Text and illustrations for each of the books in the series are checked for accuracy by an expert in the relevant field. For more information about Let's-Read-and-Find-Out Science books, write to HarperCollins Children's Books, 195 Broadway, New York, NY 10007, or visit our website at www.letsreadandfindout.com.

Let's Read-and-Find-Out Science® is a trademark of HarperCollins Publishers.

A NEST FULL OF EGGS

Library of Congress Cataloging-in-Publication Data
Jenkins, Priscilla Belz.
    A nest full of eggs / by Priscilla Belz Jenkins ; illustrated by Lizzy Rockwell.
    p.   cm. — (Let's-read-and-find-out science. Stage 1)
    ISBN 978-0-06-238193-4
    1. Robins—Juvenile literature. 2. Parental behavior in animals—Juvenile literature. 3. Eggs—Juvenile literature. [1. Robins. 2. Eggs. 3. Parental behavior in animals.] I. Rockwell, Lizzy, ill. II. Title. III. Series.
    QL696.P288J46 1995   93-43804
    598.8'42—dc20   CIP
                                                                                                                        AC

The illustrations for this book were done in pencil and watercolor on T.H. Saunders watercolor paper.

20 SCP 10 9 8
❖
Revised edition, 2015

A NEST FULL OF EGGS

Listen. "Cheer-up, cheer-up, cheer-up." That is the song of a robin. It must be spring!

Up in a tree outside my window, a pair of American robins is very busy. They are gathering dry weeds and twigs. They work carefully but quickly. It is almost time.

The female weaves the weeds and twigs together with bits of mud that dry like glue.

She adds more mud, pressing it with her breast into a cup shape.

Then she lines the bottom of the cup with a bed of soft grasses.

There. The nest is strong, safe, and snug.

Now it is ready.

Over the next few days, the female robin lays four beautiful blue eggs in the nest. She is sitting on the nest now, keeping the eggs warm. Her mate is close by. He sings loudly, warning other robins to stay away.

Inside each egg is a tiny new life. It is growing very fast. The yellow yolk is its liquid food. The clear albumen, which we call the "white" of an egg, is its watery cushion. Day after day, the mother robin sits on the eggs, patiently waiting.

3 DAYS

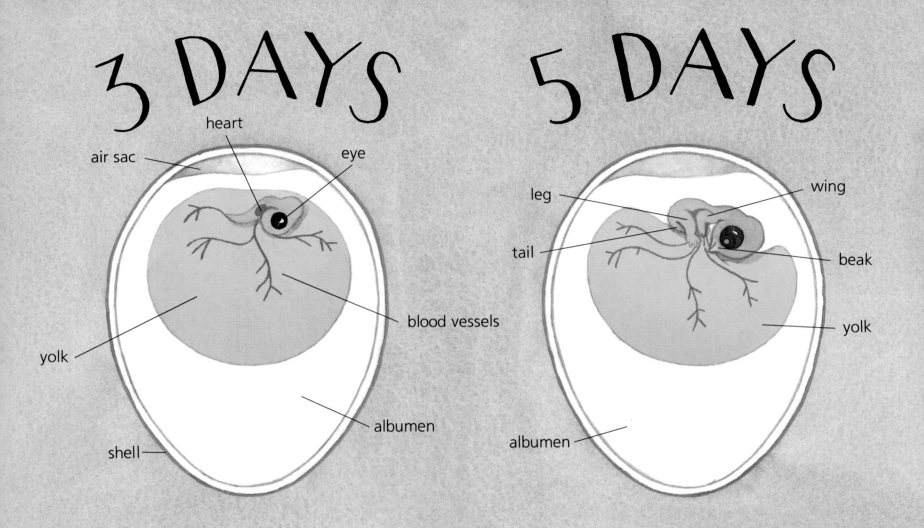

air sac

heart

eye

yolk

blood vessels

albumen

shell

5 DAYS

leg

wing

tail

beak

yolk

albumen

After three days, the life begins to look like a head, a backbone, a heart, and eyes. Already the heart is beating.

After five days, a beak, two wings, two legs, and a tail are taking shape. It is beginning to look like a baby bird in there.

8 DAYS

12 DAYS

eyelid closing over eye

shrinking yolk sac

toes

no more yolk sac

eyes are closed now— they will open after hatching

After about eight days, the robin is completely formed, right down to its toes.

By the twelfth day, the robin has grown so big, it is squeezed inside the egg. It has used up all the food and space.

Listen. "Peep. Peep. Peep-peep." A tiny beak is breaking through an eggshell. The eggs are hatching!

Crack! Out rolls a baby robin. Soon there are four wobbly little robins in the nest. Their parents feed them worms, berries, seeds, and insects. But the hungry nestlings are always peeping and squawking for more food.

15

In a few days, the baby robins open their eyes. Soft, warm down feathers begin to appear on their bodies.

Then bigger feathers grow and cover the down. They keep the robins dry and give them color and shape.

About fourteen days after hatching, the robins have grown their wing and tail feathers. These are their "flight" feathers—the feathers that they will use to fly.

Feathers are light but very strong. They are what makes birds so different from all other creatures on earth. Only birds have feathers. Feathers come in many sizes, shapes, and colors.

WE FOUND THESE IN THE YARD.

LET'S LOOK THIS ONE UP.

FEATHERS OF THE BIRDS

17

ORIOLE

FLAMINGO

BIRD OF PARADISE

CEDAR WAXWING

GUINEA FOWL

CURLEW

FINCH

PARROT

PEACOCK

HUMMINGBIRD

JUNCO

BLUE JAY

SPOTTED WOODPECKER

MANDARIN DUCK

PARAKEET

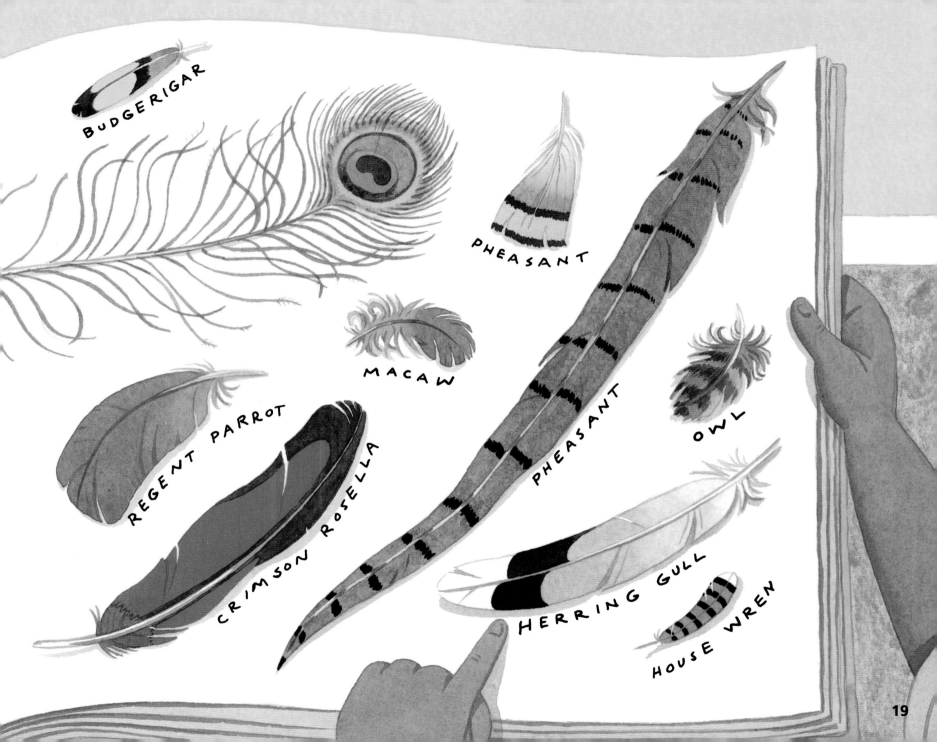

BUDGERIGAR

PHEASANT

MACAW

REGENT PARROT

CRIMSON ROSELLA

PHEASANT

OWL

HERRING GULL

HOUSE WREN

OUCH!

ROBIN

Robins, like all birds, take good care of their feathers. They comb them and straighten them with their beaks.

SPARROW TAKING A DUST BATH

And they clean them by taking baths in water or dust.

21

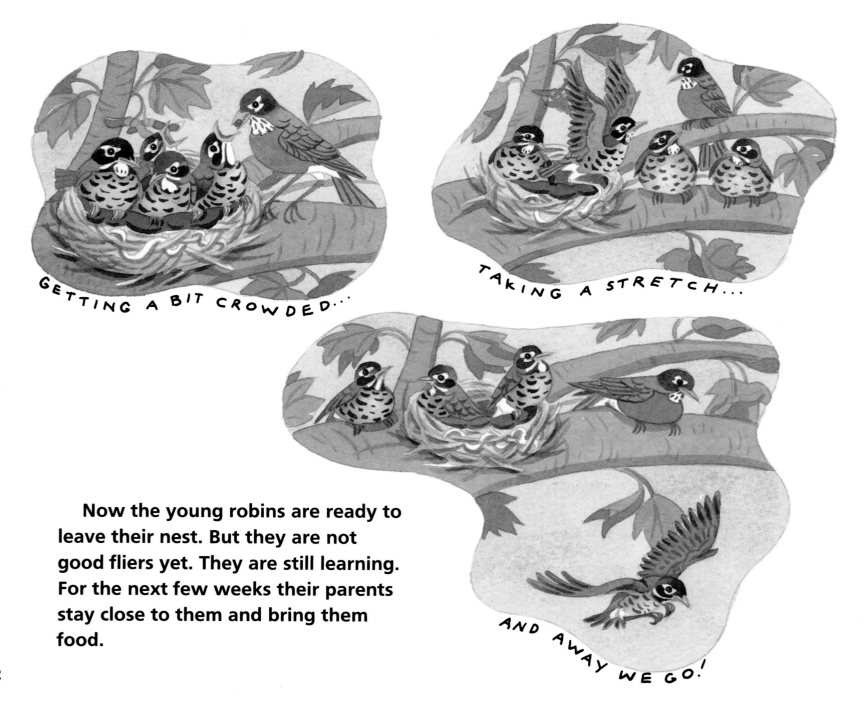

GETTING A BIT CROWDED...

TAKING A STRETCH...

AND AWAY WE GO!

Now the young robins are ready to leave their nest. But they are not good fliers yet. They are still learning. For the next few weeks their parents stay close to them and bring them food.

Soon the robins are ready to fly and hunt on their own. Now they can take care of themselves. Next spring they will find mates and have nests of their own.

23

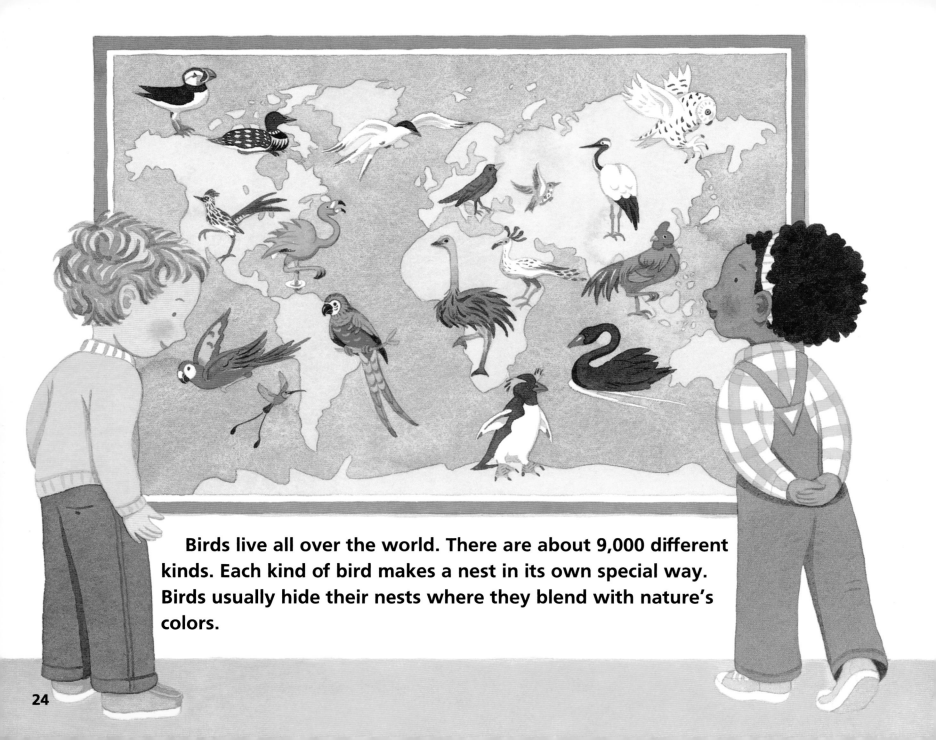

Birds live all over the world. There are about 9,000 different kinds. Each kind of bird makes a nest in its own special way. Birds usually hide their nests where they blend with nature's colors.

A bird's nest can be:

WHIP-POOR-WILL

a gathering of leaves on the forest floor

NORTHERN ORIOLE

a woven pouch

NORTHERN FLICKER

a hole in a tree

BALD EAGLE

a gigantic heap of branches

PEREGRINE FALCON

RED NECKED GREBE

a scrape on a rocky cliff top

a floating platform

a woven cup of plants and spider silk

a cup of mud

a scooped-out hollow in the sand

or even an old shoe!

You can help robins build their nests. In the spring, leave some grass clippings and bits of yarn and string in your yard. Look for robins picking them up. Watch where they go. You may be able to find their nest. Help the robins feel safe by not going too close to the nest or touching it. See if you can tell if the eggs have hatched.

YARN

HAIR

DRIED WEEDS

SHREDDED NEWSPAPER

CELLOPHANE

LOON

CROW

MURRE

EMU

ROBIN

WREN

HAWK

GULL

As summer ends in late September and the days grow shorter, the robins fly south, or migrate. They know it is time to leave. Winter is coming.

BIRDS

But the robins always return. Listen.
"Cheer-up, cheer-up, cheer-up."
Spring is here again.